The Pet Sitter

Dixie in Danger

JULIE SYKES

ILLUSTRATED BY
NATHAN REED

KINGFISHER
NEW YORK

For Alistair, Will, Tim, and Antonia

Text copyright © 2008 by Julie Sykes
Illustrations copyright © 2008 by Nathan Reed
KINGFISHER
Published in the United States by Kingfisher, an imprint of Henry Holt
and Company LLC, 175 Fifth Avenue, New York, New York 10010.
First published in Great Britain by Kingfisher Publications plc,
an imprint of Macmillan Children's Books, London.

Distributed in Canada by H. B. Fenn and Company Ltd.

Library of Congress Cataloging-in-Publication Data
has been applied for.

ISBN: 978-0-7534-6217-1

Kingfisher books are available for special promotions and premiums.
For details contact: Director of Special Markets, Holtzbrinck Publishers.

First American Edition March 2009
Printed in India
1 3 5 7 9 8 6 4 2
1TR/1008/TP/PICA/80STORA/C

CONTENTS

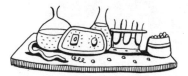

CHAPTER ONE
AN EMERGENCY

Max raced in from the backyard and through the back door before grabbing the ringing phone.

"Max?" said an impatient voice. "Max the pet sitter?"

"Yes," said Max.

Max had been pet sitting for a while now and had taken care of some unusual animals for some very strange owners.

"This is an emergency," the voice continued. "I have to go away right now, and I need someone to take care of my pet dormouse. Her name's Dixie. Can you do it?"

"Sure," said Max, checking his watch. He was taking care of a school of zebra fish, and they needed their dance class at 3:30, but there was plenty of time to go meet Dixie first. "What's your name and where do you live?"

"I'm Ivor, Ivor Gadget, and I live at thirty-six Sandy Road. Look, this really is an emergency. Can you come right away?"

"Already left!" said Max cheerfully, hanging up.

Max went upstairs to get his pet-sitter notebook. This was a small hardcover book with a picture of a whale on the front. In it Max wrote down the names of the animals that he was pet sitting and notes about their care. Max kept his notebook buried in his sock drawer. It was a simple but safe hiding place. Alice, his bossy big sister, was always nosing into his business. But she wouldn't dream of touching his socks—not for anything!

Max shoved the notebook and a pencil in his pocket and then ran downstairs to the backyard. Alice had gone outside to practice her dance moves; her legs were everywhere and her bottom was sticking up in the air. Max couldn't help himself. It was time to get Alice back for telling on him yesterday when he accidentally glued the TV remote control to the living-room carpet.

Max gave her bottom a small shove and then ran as Alice toppled headfirst into the snapdragons.

"Max!" she shrieked. "I'll get you for that!"

"You'll have to catch me first," said Max, running into the shed. He was on his bike and cycling through the yard before Alice was back on her feet.

"What is going on?" asked Mom, coming

out of the back door. "Why is Alice sitting in the flowers?"

"Maybe she thinks they'll make her smell nicer," Max said and chuckled. "I'm going out. I have another job."

"Not so fast, young man. Where and who?"

"Aw, Mom!" Max said as he stopped a safe distance from Alice, who was mouthing

threats at him. "Sandy Road, number thirty-six. Ivor Gadget wants me to take care of his dormouse."

"A dormouse!" exclaimed Mom. "I've never heard of keeping a pet dormouse. Oh well, have fun and be back by dinnertime."

"I will," said Max. "Thanks, Mom. Bye, Alice."

He waved at his sister. It felt good to get the better of her for a change!

Sandy Road wasn't far, and as Max pedaled along, he tried to imagine what type of person kept a dormouse. They weren't exactly challenging animals. From what Max could remember, dormice were nocturnal and spent up to three fourths of their life asleep.

"I bet Ivor Gadget is ancient," Max said, panting. "That's why he has a dormouse.

He'll be an old man with gray hair and wrinkles."

Max turned the corner of Sandy Road and looked at the numbers on the houses. The evens were on his left-hand side, and he counted them out.

"Thirty . . . thirty-two . . . thirty-four . . . There it is!"

Number 36 was slightly different from the other houses. Instead of having a small brick wall in front, the front yard was surrounded by a high fence. Max parked his bike and looked for a gate, but there wasn't one. The fence stretched out in an unbroken line around the entire house. So, how did he get in? Carefully, Max studied the fence. It was very high, but he was good at climbing. Max thought that if he stood on the next-door neighbor's brick wall, he could easily

climb over. Max spat on his hands and then wiped them on his shorts to give himself a better grip. He scrambled onto the brick wall, but as he reached up to the fence, he heard a sharp

click followed by a whirring noise. Looking up, Max saw a small camera on the corner of Ivor's roof, trained on him.

"Name?" asked a metallic voice.

Suspiciously, Max stared at the camera. Was this a joke?

"Name?" repeated the voice impatiently.

"Max. Max Barker, the pet sitter."

"Welcome, Max Barker."

There was an even louder click, and a gate well hidden in the fence swung open.

Max stared in amazement. "Cool!" he said.

"Hurry up," said the camera angrily. "I don't have all day."

"Neither do I!" Max said as he grabbed his bicycle and pushed it through the gate.

He was barely inside when the gate slammed shut and a second camera, mounted above the front door, focused its lens on him.

"Name?" said the camera in a squeaky metallic voice.

"What? Again?"

"No name, no entry."

"Max Barker. I'm here to pet sit. I

thought this was an emergency!"

The front door opened so suddenly that Max almost fell inside.

"It is. Don't mind the cameras. They're a little too enthusiastic at times. I'm Ivor. Thanks for coming so quickly."

"Oh!" exclaimed Max, staring up.

Ivor Gadget was not the wrinkled old man that Max had imagined. He was young and tall and had long brown hair loosely tied in a ponytail. Ivor glanced around and then quickly pulled Max inside, slamming the door behind him.

"Sorry about the security. I'm an inventor, if you hadn't already guessed. You wouldn't believe the trouble I've had with people trying to steal my ideas. But enough about me. Come and meet Dixie. You're going to love her!"

CHAPTER TWO
DIXIE VILLA

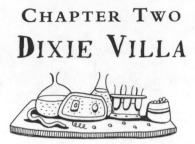

Max followed Ivor along the hallway to a room in the back of the house. On the way, he passed an elevator-like door with a strip of red and white plastic tape stretched across it. A sign on the door read, "Out of Order. Do NOT Enter."

"What's that?" asked Max curiously. "Is it an elevator?"

Ivor looked uncomfortable.

"Latest invention,"

OUT OF ORDER
DO NOT ENTER

he mumbled. "It's not finished."

"What does it do?" asked Max.

Ivor stopped and turned around to face him.

"No questions!" he said dramatically. "Look, I'm going to have to ask you to sign the Ivor Gadget Secrecy Pact. Anything you see or hear about this house is strictly private. You must not tell anyone. Not even an ant!"

"I won't say a thing," said Max, pretending to zip up his mouth. "Am I signing it in blood?"

"No need for that," said Ivor. "A pen will be fine. As long as it's not invisible ink, of course!" he said and laughed.

Max laughed, too. He'd only been joking about the blood!

"Here we are," said Ivor, opening a door. "Come and meet Dixie."

Ivor ushered Max into the room. Max stopped inside the door and stared in amazement. The room was even messier than Alice's bedroom, and that was saying something! Tall bookcases lined the walls and were crammed with everything from books to old bicycle wheels. The floor was covered with teetering piles of more books and mountains of cogs, wires, nuts, bolts, screws, computer parts, and rolls of tape. Ivor wove his way through the junk to the table.

"Dixie Villa," he said grandly.

"Wow!" Max exclaimed.

The cage looked like a two-story dollhouse, but with a wire-mesh front and a glass greenhouse instead of a roof on top. Max peered through the mesh at the rooms in the front. Each one looked like an overgrown garden in miniature. The long grass was peppered with wildflowers, shaggy bushes, and berries. Max pushed his little finger through the mesh.

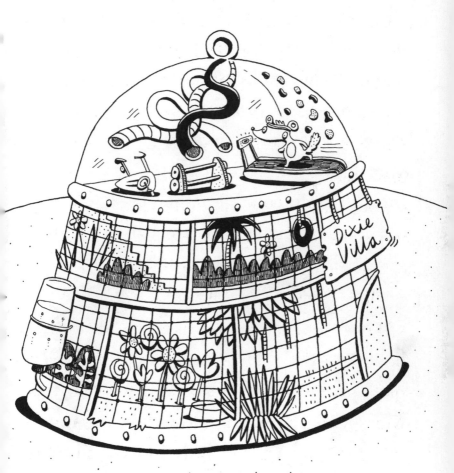

"Awesome!" he exclaimed. "It's real."

"Dixie likes the best of both worlds," said Ivor, smiling at Max's astonishment. "That's her natural environment, then there's the greenhouse on top."

A wooden staircase, carpeted with soft green moss, led to the all-glass greenhouse. In contrast to the garden rooms, the greenhouse housed a huge gymnasium with three brightly colored tunnels to slide down, a treadmill, weights, an exercise bicycle, and a

climbing wall. A small dormouse, wearing a green sweatband around her head, was pounding away on the treadmill. Suddenly, the machine slowed down, stopped, and Dixie jumped off.

"Hello," said Max, gently tapping on the glass.

Dixie fixed Max with her big black eyes. Then she turned her back on him.

"Dixie!" said Ivor in a warning tone.

The little dormouse completely ignored

him and hopped toward the stairs.

"Dixie," said Ivor again, "come and meet Max Barker, the pet sitter."

Dixie reached the top of the staircase and hesitated.

"Max is going to take care of you for the next three days. I know you don't want to stay here on your own, but it's not Max's fault, so come and say hello."

Ivor turned apologetically to Max. "Dixie's not used to being locked inside her villa. Usually she comes and goes as she pleases."

Dixie sat watching Ivor as if she was listening to him. When he'd finished, she fluffed out her orange-brown fur and stared at Ivor with big eyes. Max held his breath. Dixie looked so sad that he thought she might be about to cry!

"Dixie, don't!" Ivor pleaded. "I've made

up my mind—you're staying here while I go away."

Dixie thumped her long furry tail on the ground, and then, shooting an angry look at Max, she hopped down the staircase and out of sight.

"She likes me!" said Max sarcastically.

"It's not you," said Ivor hurriedly. "It's me she's mad at. I've never left her before, and as I said, I've never locked her up either."

"I don't mind if you don't lock her cage," said Max.

"It's not that simple," said Ivor uneasily. "Dixie's a live wire. She's always up to something. I don't want her messing with my inventions."

He checked his watch.

"Widgets! Look at the time! I have a plane to catch. I was lucky to get a seat—it was a last-minute cancellation. Quick, come to the kitchen. So much to do! There's the secrecy pact to sign and your money to sort out. I'll show you what to feed Dixie and . . . Oops, I almost forgot! I need to take a scan of your eye."

CHAPTER THREE
A NASTY SHOCK

Cycling along to Ivor Gadget's house early the next morning, Max reminded himself of his pet-sitting duties. Ivor had left all of Dixie's favorite foods. There was a bag of hazelnuts, a jar of sunflower seeds, raspberries, and apricots. It seemed like an awful lot for such a small creature, but Ivor said that Dixie had a good appetite. Max had also brought Dixie a bunch of honeysuckle that was freshly cut from his backyard. Last night, reading up about dormice, Max discovered that they liked to shred it up and sleep in it. He hoped that the present might cheer up

Dixie. She hadn't seemed happy yesterday.

Max reached the beginning of Ivor's fence and climbed off his bike.

"One, two, three, four," he counted.

When he'd taken 12 footsteps, he stopped, turned to face the fence, and then counted six hands up from the bottom. Keeping his hand on the fence, Max crouched down until his eyes were level with his hand. Then, pulling away his hand, he stared at the fence. There it was! The tiny hole that Ivor had told him about yesterday. There was a click, Max blinked, and the hidden gate swung open.

"That is so neat!"

Max exclaimed.

Instead of a key, the doors opened by recognizing people's eyes. Yesterday Ivor had scanned the inside of Max's eye so that he could get in, too.

Leaving his bicycle just inside the gate, Max repeated the whole thing at the front door, shouting, "Hi, Dixie. It's only me!" as he stepped inside.

The house had an empty feel. Maybe Dixie was still asleep. Max hurried down the hallway, glancing curiously at the elevator-like door as he passed. It was an odd thing to have in a house, and Max wondered what it was for. Pushing open the door to Dixie's room, Max threaded his way around the piles of junk. Dixie Villa seemed even more impressive this morning. Max decided that Ivor must be very fond of the dormouse to build her such an amazing home. Dixie was not in the gym or any of the rooms in the front. Max lay the honeysuckle on the table in front of Dixie Villa and called out, "Hi, Dixie. It's Max!"

Nothing, not even a friendly squeak! The silence worried Max.

"Dixie, are you in there? It's breakfast time. Come and say hello, and then I'll get you something to eat. I wonder what you'd like. How about an apricot and some raspberries?"

There was still no sign of Dixie.

"Good choice. Apricot it is," said Max, reaching out to unclip the tiny water bottle that was fastened to the outside of Dixie's cage.

The bottle had a small metal drinking spout that poked in through the cage bars.

Max was lifting it out when the spout whipped around and blasted him with cold water.

"Eek!" he shrieked, dropping the bottle onto the table. "How on earth did that happen?" Wiping the water from his eyes, Max was sure he heard a squeaky giggle.

"Ouch!"

Something hit him on the nose. It was a

sunflower seed, and it was quickly followed by more. Max scrabbled around, picking them up and flicking them back. It was a waste of time. Dixie was too well hidden in the overgrown garden for the seeds to hit her, but Max enjoyed flicking the seeds anyway.

After a little while, the missiles stopped. Over the top of a small bush came a twig with a white flower speared on the end.

"Truce!" shouted a squeaky voice.

Max stared in amazement as Dixie slowly peeked out from behind the bush.

A talking dormouse! Was this a trick, too?

"Truce," said Dixie angrily. "Are you deaf or what?"

Max recovered himself.

"No, I just didn't realize that you could talk. You never said a word yesterday when Ivor was here."

"There was nothing to say," said Dixie. "Truce? Will you stop fighting me?"

"You started it!" Max exclaimed.

"It's not my fault."

"Well, it wasn't mine!"

"Being locked up is doing funny things to me. I'm going crazy in here. You have to let me out."

Dixie's long black whiskers quivered. Max held his breath as she slowly edged out into the open. Her bright black eyes were sad. "Please?" she said.

"Dixie, I can't do that. Ivor said I had to keep you locked up for your own safety."

"Phooey!" exclaimed Dixie. "I never mess with any of his inventions! Make them better, yes. Invent stuff that Ivor's not even thought of, yes. But mess things up? No, NEVER!"

Max was torn. Dixie was used to having her freedom, and it felt mean to cage her, but Max was responsible for her safety. What if he disobeyed Ivor and something went wrong—how would he feel then?

"It's for only three days. You'll be out before you know it. I'll spend the day with you, if you'd like. Keep you company."

"Phooey! I'd rather keep my own company," Dixie said with a growl.

"Suit yourself," said Max. "The offer stands if you change your mind. I'll get your breakfast."

He picked up the water bottle from the table.

"Neat trick, by the way. How did you get it to squirt me?"

Dixie didn't answer. Sighing to himself, Max took the bottle to the kitchen to refill it. Ivor had left the apricots in a bowl, and Max gently squeezed them, choosing the softest one for Dixie's breakfast. He cut it in half, removed the pit, and piled fresh raspberries on top. The whole thing looked so tasty that Max could have eaten it himself. He washed his sticky hands before proudly carrying the water and food back to Dixie.

"Breakfast, and I brought you some honeysuckle, too."

Max hadn't expected an answer, but when he looked into the cage, he got a nasty shock. Dixie lay on her side in the long grass, eyes closed, tail sticking out like a flagpole. She was very still. Too still. Max stepped closer.

CHAPTER FOUR
THE CHASE

"**D**ixie? Dixie, are you all right?"

Max threw down her breakfast and wrenched open the front of the cage. A jumble of thoughts whizzed through his mind. Dixie was so still that she didn't seem to be breathing. Had she died? But how? She'd been fine a few minutes ago. Unless their discussion had given her a heart attack. Max thought that he was having one, too. His heart was jumping like a kangaroo. What should he do? Last quarter at school, Max's class had been taught how to give mouth-to-mouth resuscitation. It was a way of breathing for someone if they couldn't do it themselves. Could you give a dormouse mouth-to-mouth? Max decided to try. He knew that he needed to be careful. Dixie was so little that if he breathed too hard, she might blow up like a balloon!

Dixie lay still as, with trembling fingers, Max reached inside the cage to lift her out. His fingers touched her thick orange fur. *Thwap!* Dixie smacked Max with her tail.

"Sucker!" she squeaked, jumping up and leaping to freedom.

"Dixie!" bellowed Max. "That's not funny."

Dixie scampered across the table, scattering the bunch of honeysuckle as she ran down to the floor. Max leaped after her, knocking over piles of junk in his rush to stop her from escaping. He would have caught her if he hadn't tripped over a broken guitar that sent him crashing to the ground.

"Mouse brains!" said Max, pulling his foot out of the hole in the middle. The guitar's broken strings snaked around his legs, holding him tightly. Max pulled them away and then scrambled after Dixie. He was in time to see her fat orange tail disappear around the curve in the stairs. Max climbed up after her and found himself in a room that was even more cluttered than the one he'd just left.

"Dixie?"

Max leaned against the doorjamb and scanned the messy room. And his mom thought she had problems with Alice! You could hide a rhinoceros in here and nobody would ever know.

"Come on, Dixie. The joke's over."

Dixie didn't answer. No surprises there!

There was another elevator-like door in this room, with a single strip of red and white plastic tape across it. Max did some quick calculating. It was directly above the one downstairs. So it *was* an elevator! He noticed a keypad to the side of the door

with two large buttons marked "P" and "F." What did that mean? Max grinned. Inventors! They were all the same. Definitely a screw loose!

There was a rustle from the other side of the room. Max spun around. The noise had come from under the window. Silently, he tiptoed toward it. Suddenly, an orange ball of fur broke cover and shot across the room toward the door. Turning, Max dived, his fingers closing around Dixie's tail as he landed.

"Gotcha!"

But he hadn't! Max was left holding a clump of soft orange fur as Dixie scampered away. A crazy chase followed—Dixie whizzing around the room and Max crashing after her through mounds of junk. Max was determined to catch

Dixie and dived like a football player each time the dormouse popped into sight. A bead of sweat ran down his nose and his heart was banging like crazy. He paused for a

moment to catch his breath and then leaped up as Dixie shot past. Halfway across the room, Dixie disappeared into a bundle of old  clothes. The clothes jumped and wiggled like live animals and then suddenly stopped moving. Max crept closer. A striped sweater caught his eye. Was that a dormouse-shaped bump in its sleeve? Silently, Max squatted down. Yes, he was sure it was Dixie! Max prodded the bump. The sweater squeaked and the bump ran down its sleeve. Max cupped his hands and, as Dixie ran out through the cuff, sprang.

"Gotcha!" he cried. He skidded across the floor, crashed through the red and white tape, and smacked into the elevator buttons. The elevator door burst open, and Max hurtled inside, letting go of Dixie as he rolled across the floor. Dixie struggled up and then stared around in horror.

"Quick!" she squeaked. "We have to get out of here!"

The elevator doors were closing.

Dixie ran toward them, shrieking, "Out, NOW!"

Max could see that they wouldn't make it in time, so he looked for a button to hold open the doors. All elevators had one, so where was it? He ran his hands along the wall in case he was missing something and found a crease in the surface. He felt it with his finger. The crease made a square with an indent at the top. Max stuck his finger into the indent and pulled. The square of wall opened, revealing the elevator's controls: four buttons and a circular hole with a wire poking out. The buttons were marked "P," "F," <>, and ><. The symbols were the same as the ones in the elevator at the mall. Max couldn't guess what the "P" and "F" meant, but he knew that <> would open the doors and >< would close them.

The elevator doors snapped shut. Frantically, Max pushed the button marked <>, but it was too late. The elevator was moving.

CHAPTER FIVE
A RIDE IN AN ELEVATOR

They were going up, which was strange because Ivor's house had only two floors. After a few seconds, the elevator stopped. Relieved, Max pressed the button to open the doors, and when nothing happened, he pressed it again. Without warning, the elevator threw itself sideways. Max grabbed for the handrail and was glad that he had. Now the elevator was spinning, faster and faster, making his skinny body shake and his teeth chatter together.

"Hold on!" shouted Dixie, climbing onto Max's foot and sinking her claws into his shoelace.

"Great idea!" said Max. Like he was going to do anything else! He was spinning so violently that he could hardly breathe. He wanted to pick up Dixie, to make sure that she was safe, but when he tried, he found that the force was too great and he couldn't move.

The spinning went on until Max could hardly bear it, and then at last the elevator slowed down and finally stopped moving. "Whoa!" said Max.

He stood up for a second, too dizzy to move, but then as he reached up to open the doors . . .

"Eek!"

Faster than a stone hurled from the top of a skyscraper, the elevator plummeted. Max's stomach met his feet, and then suddenly, without even slowing down, the elevator stopped again. Max almost bit his tongue as it bounced up and down as if it had landed on an enormous trampoline. Up and down went the elevator, until gradually it stopped and the doors slid open.

"Dixie, are you okay?"

 There was a muffled squeak. Dixie was clinging onto Max's shoelace with her teeth as well as both front paws. Max staggered

through the doors, blinking in the bright light. "That," he said, "was some ride!"

"Don't mind me," Dixie squeaked angrily. She jumped from Max's foot. "You call yourself a pet sitter? You almost squashed me with those great big feet."

"Sorry!" Max bent down to pick her up, but she slapped him away with her tail.

"You will be!" she exclaimed. "Ivor's going to kill you when he finds out that you've taken his elevator. You're the one who needs to be locked up, not me!"

"What? This is your fault!" said Max. "I'm here only because I was chasing you. Where are we, anyway? Is this Ivor's backyard?"

He looked around and saw neatly trimmed bushes, colorful plants, stone statues, and a rectangular pond with a dolphin fountain in the middle and mosaic tiles around the edges.

"Nice," said Max, "if you like that type of thing. A little too ancient Rome for me. There's nowhere to kick a ball around."

"Ancient Rome?" asked Dixie.

"Yep, we studied it in history last quarter. We had a Roman day and wore togas, a little bit like that boy over there . . ." Max's voice trailed off.

"Hide," hissed Dixie, diving under a bush.

Max wiggled in after her. The boy was in a hurry and luckily didn't notice the elevator nestled between two small willowy trees. He muttered to himself as he struggled to carry a huge basket full of ripe cherries. Max's stomach rumbled. Breakfast seemed like a long time ago.

Dixie, who hadn't eaten her breakfast, was obviously thinking the same thing. "Come

on," she said once the boy had passed. "Let's go find where those cherries came from."

"Hang on!" said Max. "Dixie, where are we exactly?"

"Not too sure," said Dixie. "Ancient Rome sounds about right. Impossible to say without looking at the time dial."

"You're saying that's a time elevator?" squeaked Max. "I don't believe you!"

"Excuse me, did I say time elevator? Silly me! I meant that we've taken the elevator to Ivor's attic. Look around, genius. What do you see?"

Max stuck his head out of the bush and gazed around, noticing a low villa with high windows and a veranda on the other side of the pond. Just then two girls in short white tunics hurried through the garden with a basket of tomatoes and disappeared inside the house.

"It *is* ancient Rome!" Max exclaimed. "Unreal!"

"Well, I'm real and I need food," said Dixie. "Come on."

Max hesitated. The responsible pet sitter side of him said to get back into the elevator and go straight home. But the curious,

adventure-seeking side was dying to see a bit more of ancient Rome.

"Hurry up," said Dixie. "You'll think

better on a full stomach."

Max crumpled. The cherries had looked delicious. Surely it wouldn't hurt to have a little look around? It was the chance of a lifetime, and he'd regret it if he didn't take it. He scrambled out of the bush and hurried after Dixie.

"What did you mean about thinking better on a full stomach?" he asked.

Dixie didn't answer, and Max got the feeling that she was hiding something, but before he could question her, they reached the orchard.

"Wow!" said Max, impressed by the fruit-laden trees. "Where should we start?"

CHAPTER SIX
DIXIE DISAPPEARS

A short ladder was propped against one tree, and next to it was a huge basket full of shiny red cherries. Dixie scampered up the side of the basket and began eating. Max had never picked cherries before, so he climbed halfway up the ladder and ate them straight from the tree. They tasted delicious! Sticky, sweet juice squirted over him as he bit into the soft flesh. He was so busy eating, and seeing how far he could spit the pits, that he didn't hear the soft steps approaching. He almost fell off the ladder in surprise when a voice shouted up

at him, "Don't let the master catch you!
He'll chop off your hand for that."

Max's stomach clenched. Suddenly the
fruit tasted sour in his mouth.

"You're new, aren't you? Where are you
from? You must be foreign with clothes like
that!"

"I'm not the one wearing the dress!" Max
exclaimed.

The boy gave him an odd look. "There's
no need to be unfriendly."

"I wasn't," said
Max, trying not to
laugh.

Max always
laughed when he
was nervous, and it
often got him into
trouble. "I'm just . . .

um . . . I'm not from around here,"
he added.

"Well, that's obvious! You're not one of
those barbarians, are you? Are you one of the
Vandals?" the boy asked, looking a little
nervous.

Max smiled at him and was wondering how
to answer when the boy added, "Enough
talking! There's no time for idleness with a
banquet to prepare. Come. You can give
me a hand with the basket. It's needed in
the kitchen."

Max stared at the boy. What should he do?
He didn't want to go to the kitchen, where
there would be a lot of people and more
chance of discovery. Slowly, as he backed
down the ladder, a simple plan formed in his
head. He would grab Dixie and make a run
for it back to the elevator. But Dixie had

disappeared. Max stared at the basket. Was she hiding among the cherries or had she climbed out and gone somewhere else?

"Hurry up," said the boy. "We'll get a beating if we're gone too long."

There was nothing else to do. Max took one handle of the basket and reluctantly helped the boy carry it back to the kitchen. He didn't need to worry about being discovered. The kitchen was hot and crowded, with too many people rushing around.

"Put that there and then go fetch me some lettuce," snapped a hassled-looking cook wearing a three-quarter-length tunic. "And be quick."

Max stared at the basket of cherries. This was a good chance to escape, but where was Dixie? Max couldn't leave without the dormouse.

"I'm going to the garden to get some lettuce," he said loudly, in case Dixie was in the basket and could hear him.

The cook eyed him suspiciously.

"Just get on with it," she snapped.

Max stared at the basket once more and saw that the cherries were moving. They rolled over one another like glossy red marbles as something pushed its way through them. A twitching nose followed by long whiskers appeared.

"About time," said Max, bending down and scooping Dixie up into his hand. "Been enjoying yourself, have you?"

"Keep your tail on," said Dixie. "It was no picnic in there."

"No?" Max said with a chuckle, wiping a smear of cherry juice from Dixie's face. "Of course it wasn't."

"Hey!" shouted a short girl in a dirty tunic, pointing an accusing finger at Max. "The new boy's got a fatty mouse. He stole it from the pot."

"Fatty mouse! Huh!" squeaked Dixie indignantly.

Max burst out laughing, but the kitchen fell silent and everyone stared at him. *Bang!* The hassled-looking cook slammed her knife into the table.

"No one steals from my kitchen!" she roared. "Here, boy, now!"

"Stealing?" Max shot a furious look at the girl in the filthy tunic. "I wasn't stealing. I caught a dormouse eating the cherries, and I was putting her outside."

"Why?" asked the cook, staring at Max.

Max returned her gaze without even blinking. "Because that's where she belongs."

"You're new, aren't you? Then I'll give you the benefit of the doubt. Give me the fatty mouse. It belongs in this pot."

Max let out a tiny sigh of relief as the cook pointed to a large clay pot high up on a shelf. Max's brain buzzed as he tried to remember why the ancient Romans would keep dormice in a clay pot.

"Galloping gladiators!" he hissed, suddenly recalling the reason.

Dormice, or fatty mice as they called them, were a delicacy in Roman times. They were kept in clay pots until they were nice and plump, and then they were cooked. If he handed over Dixie, she would be roasted and eaten at the banquet. Max closed his hand protectively around his little friend. Difficult as she was, he couldn't help liking her. Besides, he was the pet sitter. There was no way he was handing over his latest responsibility.

"Hurry, boy!" snapped the woman.

"I'll put her back," said Max, stalling for time.

"You! You're far too short to reach," the woman said, laughing. "Give the fatty mouse to me and then go fetch the lettuce."

Max reached toward her and then suddenly gave a bloodcurdling yell and gently dropped Dixie onto the floor.

"Ouch! She bit me!"

Clutching his finger, Max gave an award-winning performance of pretending to be in pain.

"Clumsy oaf!" shrieked the cook. "Don't just stand there. Catch it!"

Dirty Tunic took off, shoving past Max to chase after Dixie.

"Tattletale," Max muttered, thinking that he'd like to shove her in a pot for roasting.

Several of the younger slaves also put down their tools to join in the chase, while the older ones shook their heads and continued working. Desperately, Max elbowed people out of the way. He had to reach Dixie before anyone else did. But Dixie was whizzing around and around the kitchen like a firecracker, and no one could get near her. She darted across the feet of a boy who then slipped on a tomato and crashed to the ground. A second boy tripped over him,

pulling Dirty Tunic down with him.

"Awesome!" cheered Max, avoiding the pileup.

Dixie squeezed in behind a tall clay jar as the slaves on the floor struggled to get up.

"Where did it go?"

"It was there a minute ago."

"It went that way."

Max sidled over to the jar and squatted down beside it.

"Dixie," he hissed, "it's me, Max. Climb onto my hand and I'll get you out of here."

"No," said Dixie angrily. "There's a whole bunch of my relatives in that pot. I'm not leaving without freeing them."

"You're going to try to rescue them? Dixie, you can't! It's way too dangerous. We have to get back to the elevator before there's real trouble."

"Then go without me."

"Don't tempt me," said Max.

"I'm not going anywhere until I've saved my relatives," said Dixie. "You wouldn't."

Max thought about his family, and an image of Alice making fun of him in front of all her friends floated into his head. Would he risk his life to save Alice? Annoying as she was, Max knew that he probably would.

"All right," he said. "Climb onto my hand and I'll help you rescue them."

CHAPTER SEVEN
STUCK IN TIME

Dixie clambered onto Max's hand, and he closed his fingers around her soft little body. Half a second later, he was surrounded by Dirty Tunic and a bunch of slaves.

"Where did the mouse go?" asked one. "Did you see it?"

"It went that way," said Max.

He chuckled as the slaves rushed to the other side of the kitchen, and then he casually sauntered over to the shelf where the earthenware pot stood. No one noticed. The older slaves were busy with their work. The younger ones were searching for Dixie in a basket of tomatoes. Max pulled himself up onto the wooden table directly below the shelf. The table wobbled, and Max grabbed at the shelf to steady himself. The clay pot was heavy and Max needed both hands to lift it down. He was so busy trying not to drop it that when the table wobbled again, Max fell back, landing on his bottom with the clay pot in his lap. His hand flew to his pocket and felt for Dixie, and then he grinned as she tickled him with her tail. That was close. He'd have to be more careful. The jar would have given Dixie more than a headache if it had landed on her!

Dirty Tunic was crawling around on the floor. If she looked up now, she would see Max sitting on the table. Quietly, Max lay the jar on its side and eased off the lid. He angled the jar away from himself, expecting the dormice to rush out, but nothing happened. Max stuck his hand inside the jar, and his fingers sank into a mass of velvety bodies. Even then they didn't stir.

"Dixie, help me," Max whispered.

Dixie wiggled out of his pocket, climbed onto the jar, and stuck her head inside. She began squeaking very fast in dormouse language. Seconds later, the jar erupted with orange fur balls as a dozen fat dormice scampered to safety.

As they fled, they knocked the lid to the ground, and it smashed on the stone floor. Dirty Tunic spun around.

"You!" she cried, standing up. "You've let all the fatty mice go."

Max grabbed Dixie and scrambled down from the table, but the cook had seen him.

"Clumsy!" she yelled, boxing Max on the ear. "Catch them now or I'll be roasting you instead."

Max fled across the kitchen and outside. Dirty Tunic followed as Max dodged around the statues to the part of the garden where they'd left the elevator.

"Stop!" cried Dirty Tunic.

"In your dreams!" shouted Max.

The elevator was where he'd remembered—sandwiched between two willowy trees. Max threw himself at it, slamming his hand on the buttons outside. The doors slid open. Max ran in, flipped open the hidden control panel, and pressed the >< button.

"Hurrah!" he cheered as the elevator closed.

"What is this place?" asked a voice.

Max spun around. Dirty Tunic had followed him into the elevator.

"Get out," he said, shoving her backward.

"I won't."

"Get out!" yelled Max, shoving her harder.

Dirty Tunic leaned against the elevator doors. "I can't. The door's disappeared. This place is so strange."

"Bye-bye," said Max.

He pushed a button, the doors slid open, and Dirty Tunic fell backward into the garden.

"You can't hide in there forever!" she shouted as the doors closed again.

Max slumped against the elevator wall to catch his breath.

"Dixie, what do we press to get home?" he asked. "Is it the

'F' button? 'F' for *future*, right?"

Dixie crouched on the floor, and her long black whiskers trembled.

"It's not that simple," she said.

"Well, make it simple!" yelled Max. "We don't have much time."

Dixie quivered. "I can't. I was going to tell you earlier."

"Tell me what?" Max felt uneasy. What hadn't Dixie told him?

"We can't get back. The elevator isn't finished. The time dial needs a pointer so that you can pick the exact date you want to travel to. Ivor's friend Tor was making a special one carved from an oak tree. Ivor was so excited when Tor e-mailed to say that the pointer was ready. That's why he went away, to pick up the pointer."

Max stared at Dixie in disbelief. After a

minute, he asked, "So how did we get here?"

"Luck of the draw," Dixie replied. "Pressing 'F' takes you somewhere into the future. Pressing 'P' takes you back into the past. You just can't set an exact date."

"Great!" exploded Max. "Why didn't you tell this me before?"

"You were more interested in going off to

find the cherries," said Dixie.

"What? The cherries were your idea," Max said. His green eyes narrowed into tiny slits.

"All right!" said Dixie, sounding a little bit embarrassed. "I decided to keep it for later. I think better on a full stomach."

Max felt his heart beat faster as he thought about their predicament. They could be stuck in the wrong time forever.

"Okay," he said slowly. His heart was still racing and he felt slightly out of breath. "What happens now?"

"We press the 'F' button and hope for the best. Wherever we go, it can't be worse than this place." Dixie shuddered. "Roasted dormouse! That's bad!"

It wasn't the answer Max wanted, but Dixie was right. Traveling closer to their own time had to be less dangerous than being stuck in ancient Roman times. Then Max had an idea. What if they had a makeshift time-dial pointer? Could that get them back to their own time?

"What does the pointer look like? Could we make one?"

"It has a round bottom and a long pointed stick like a speedometer in a car," said Dixie.

Max glanced at Dixie's fat little body and her long tail and then grinned.

"No way!" squeaked Dixie, reading his mind. "You are not using me!"

A sudden pounding on the door made Max and Dixie jump.

"Open up!" bellowed a man's voice.

The pounding continued until the elevator doors burst open. A surprised-looking man in a long white tunic stared in. Dirty Tunic was with him, and she was fiddling with the elevator controls.

"That's him," she said smugly.

Quickly, Max pushed the >< button, and the doors slid closed again. He kept his finger on the button to keep them shut, ignoring the angry shouts from outside.

Think! What could be used for a makeshift time-dial pointer? Unusually, Max's pockets were empty except for his pet-sitter notebook and a pencil. Max stared around the elevator, but besides himself and Dixie, it was completely empty. Then he had an idea. His pencil would make a good pointer, and the button on his pants was round! Using his free hand, Max unfastened the button and tried to pull it off. The button was stitched so firmly in place that it didn't even move.

"Dixie," said Max, "can you nibble this free for me?"

"Good idea," said Dixie. "You're going to use it for a pointer."

Quickly, she scampered up Max's leg and sunk her teeth into the thread. Max giggled.

"That tickles!"

The pounding on the door grew more violent.

"Open up. Open up at once or I'll feed you to the lions!"

"Careful!" Max said, chuckling. "Your whiskers are *soooo* tickly!"

"Paaa!" Dixie spat out a mouthful of thread and then triumphantly passed Max the button. "It goes in that hole," she said.

"I know," said Max, having already figured out that the hole in the control panel was where the time-dial pointer should be.

Max threaded the button through the dangling wire with his free hand. It was way too small, but it would have to do. Next, he fastened the pencil to it, using the end of the wire. He gave it a twist, cheering as the pencil spun around.

"Ready?" he asked Dixie.

"Ready," she agreed, climbing into his pocket.

Max thought for a

moment. He wasn't sure how far to turn the pencil. Roman times had been around 2,000 years ago, so he'd better give it a good twist. The pounding outside was replaced by a metallic-sounding twang, as if someone was attacking the elevator with an ax. Hurriedly, Max turned the pencil three fourths of the way around and then slammed his hand on the "F" button. For a second, nothing happened, but then the elevator suddenly shot sideways and then upward.

"Hurrah!" cheered Max, grabbing the handrail as the spinning began.

CHAPTER EIGHT
INTO THE FUTURE

The spinning lasted longer this time. Max gripped the handrail until his hands were numb from holding on. He could feel Dixie's warm little body in his pocket, and he hoped that she was all right. When at last the spinning stopped, Max waited, ready for the sudden plunge downward. But this time, the elevator was full of surprises.

"Eeeek!" he shouted as they shot upward.

Max wasn't sure which was worse: the feeling of falling or this new feeling of whizzing into space. Neither, he decided. It was this part: the sudden jolt as the elevator bounced itself to a standstill. This was a hundred times worse than anything else. Max's bones felt as if they were about to come crashing through his skin. He closed his eyes until at last the elevator stilled and the doors finally opened.

"Phew!" he cried, seeing that they were downstairs in Ivor's hallway. "We made it! How lucky was that?"

Eagerly, Dixie scrambled out of Max's pocket.

"Listen!" Max caught her as she scampered down his leg. "What's that noise?"

Cautiously, he stuck his head out of the elevator and then quickly pulled it back in. Who was the old man with the long gray hair shuffling down the hallway? Ivor hadn't said that anyone else would be visiting Dixie.

Coughing and wheezing, the man shuffled closer.

"Who's there?" he called out. "I thought I heard something. Who is it?"

"Ivor!" squeaked Dixie. "What happened?"

Something clicked in Max's brain.

"Silly dormouse!" he exclaimed. "We've overshot. We've traveled into the future."

Quickly, he shut the elevator doors, and then, reaching up, he twisted the pencil back a little and hit the "P" button.

"Let's hope this docs it," he muttered as the elevator began to spin.

Anxiously, Max waited. What if he'd turned the pointer too far? They could be traveling backward and forward forever. Seconds later, the ride was over and the elevator doors opened. Tentatively, Max looked out.

They were back in Ivor's house, in the upstairs room where they had started. "We did it! We're home!" Max cheered. He checked his watch—they'd been gone an hour, although it seemed like much longer.

Pulling up his pants, which were slipping down his skinny waist, he triumphantly carried Dixie out of the elevator.

CHAPTER NINE
HOME AGAIN

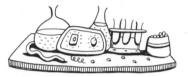

Max and Dixie were having a water fight with Dixie's water bottles. Dixie had shown Max how to make the spout twist around and squirt water, but she was still getting the better of him since she was an expert at hiding.

"Mouse-eye!" shouted Dixie, leaping out from behind a tire and blasting Max in the face.

"I'll get you for that," Max said and laughed, wiping water from his eyes.

"Not if I get you first!" shrieked Dixie, blasting Max again.

Max ducked and fired back, soaking

Dixie's long furry tail as she raced behind an old computer.

"Mouse-eye!" he yelled.

"Hold fire!" Dixie's head popped around the computer, her ears twitching.

"Yeah, right!" Max said, laughing, and blasted her again. "I'm not that stupid!"

"No, really. That was the door. Quick, Ivor's home!"

Dixie ran back to her cage. Max dropped his water bottle and frantically mopped up the mess. He managed to clean up most of the water before Ivor came into the room.

"Hello," said Max, stuffing a wad of wet tissues into his pocket.

"Hello," said Ivor, looking around. "It's a

little damp in here. Is everything all right?"

"Everything's fine," said Max.

"Couldn't be finer!" called Dixie from her villa.

Ivor looked at them both suspiciously.

"Good to see you two are so friendly," he said eventually. "Dixie behaved herself, did she? She wasn't talking to you when I left."

"Dixie's been very good," said Max.

"What about him?" Ivor asked Dixie.

"The best pet sitter ever," said Dixie.

"I knew he would be," Ivor said as he dumped his suitcase on top of the broken guitar and then let Dixie out of her cage.

"Did you have an enjoyable trip?" Max asked politely.

"Oh, yes," Ivor said,

and his eyes flicked to his suitcase. "The trip went very well. The time just flew by. I can't believe I've been away for three whole days. I'll be an old man, little and bald, before I know it."

Max and Dixie chuckled.

"Old maybe, but bald . . . I don't think so," Dixie said and winked at Max.

Ivor tweaked his long ponytail.

"Maybe not bald," he agreed.

"Old and gray?" suggested Max.

Ivor gave him a sharp look, but Max was already hurrying toward the door.

"I'll be going, then!" he called. "See you around, Dixie. Bye, Ivor."

"Bye, Max," said Dixie. "See you sometime in the future, maybe!"

Me and Dixie!